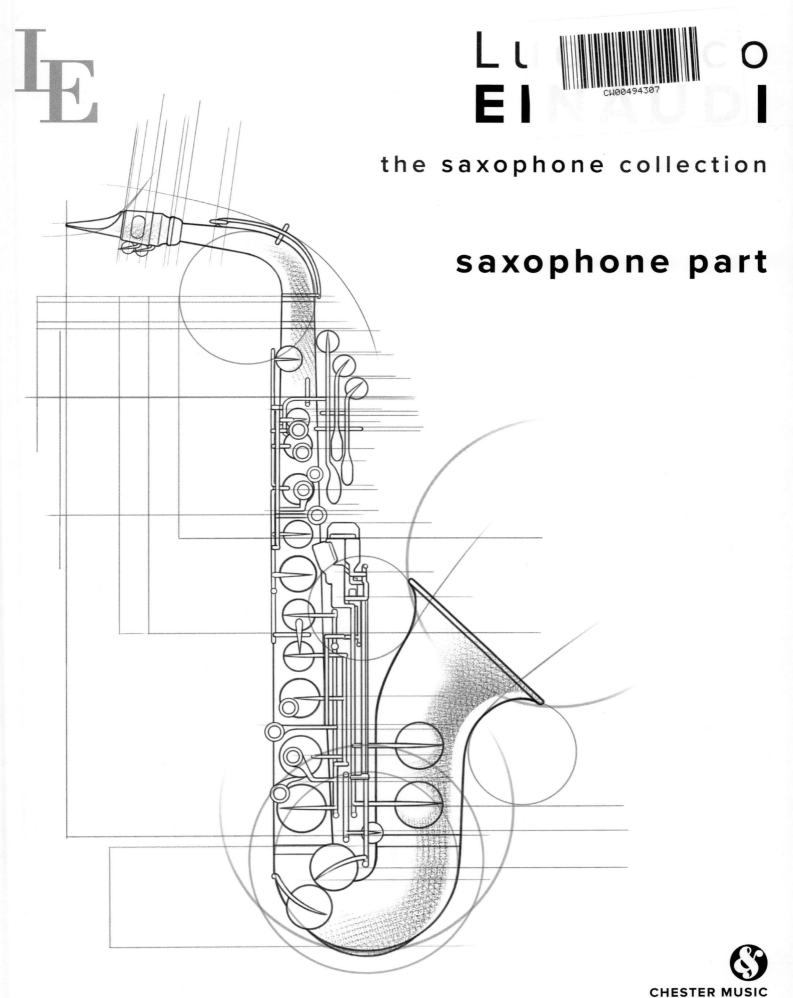

L E

Ludovico EINAUDI

the saxophone collection

saxophone part

CHESTER MUSIC
part of The Music Sales Group
London/New York/Paris/Sydney/Copenhagen/Berlin/Madrid/Hong Kong/Tokyo

Published by

Chester Music
part of The Music Sales Group
14-15 Berners Street, London W1T 3LJ, UK.

Exclusive Distributors:
Music Sales Limited
Distribution Centre, Newmarket Road,
Bury St Edmunds, Suffolk IP33 3YB, UK.

Music Sales Corporation
180 Madison Avenue, 24th Floor,
New York NY 10016, USA.

Music Sales Pty Limited
Level 4, Lisgar House,
30-32 Carrington Street,
Sydney, NSW 2000 Australia.

Order No. CH85030-01
ISBN 978-1-78558-325-4
This book © Copyright 2017 Chester Music Limited.
All Rights Reserved.

Project managed by Sam Lung.
Compiled and edited by Sam Lung, Louise Unsworth and James Welland.
Arrangements by Ludovico Einaudi, Alistair Watson and Sam Lung.
Music engraved by Sarah Lofthouse, SEL Music Art Ltd.
Audio mixed and mastered by Jonas Persson.
Saxophone recorded by Sam Corkin.
Piano recorded by Ben Dawson.
Design by Ruth Keating.
Cover illustration by Sergio Sandoval.
With special thanks to the English Session Orchestra contracted by Jojo Arvanitis.

Printed in the EU.

www.musicsales.com

Contents

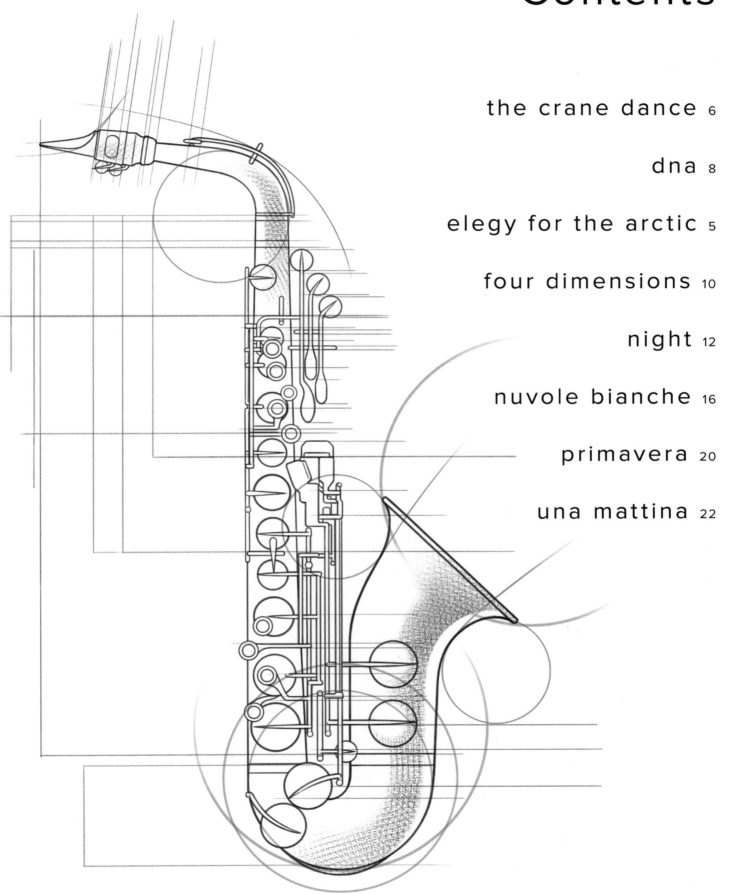

alto saxophone solo

elegy for the arctic

LUDOVICO **EINAUDI**

the crane dance

LUDOVICO **EINAUDI**

dna

LUDOVICO **EINAUDI**

four dimensions

LUDOVICO **EINAUDI**

alto saxophone solo

night

LUDOVICO **EINAUDI**

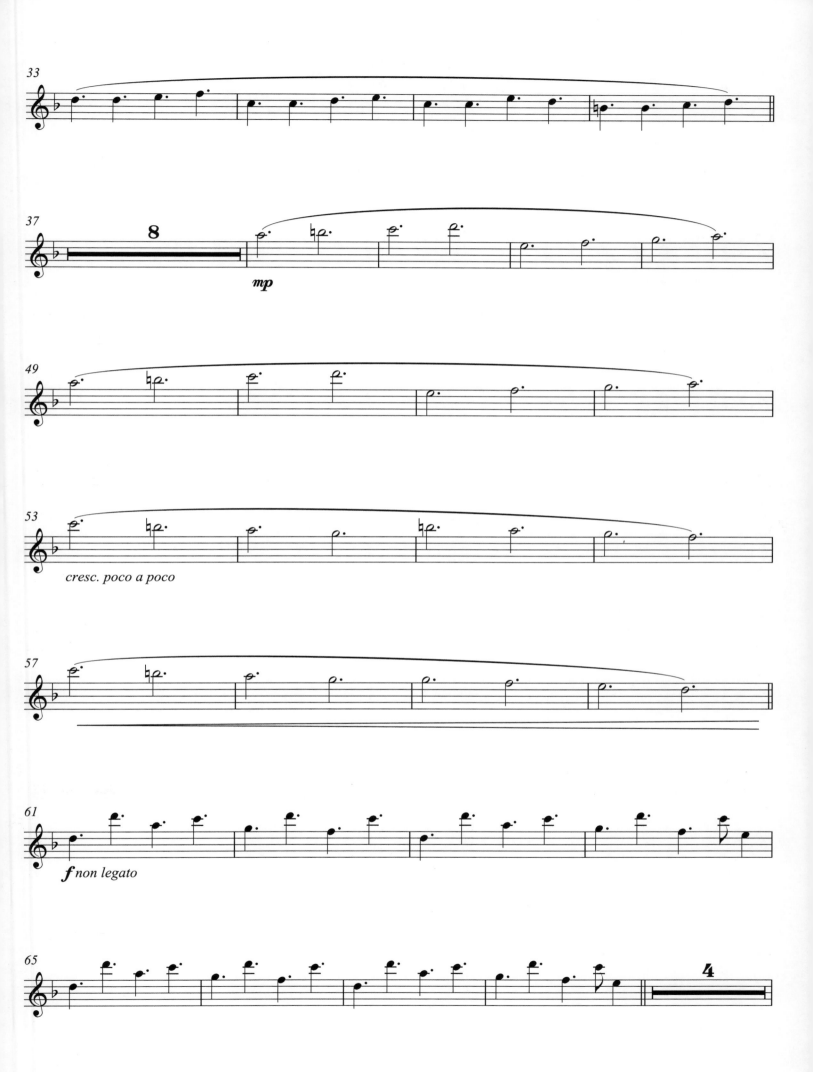

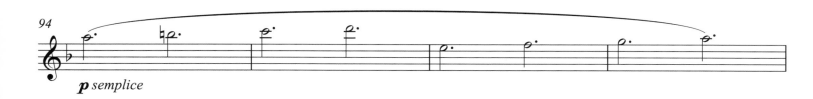

nuvole bianche

LUDOVICO **EINAUDI**

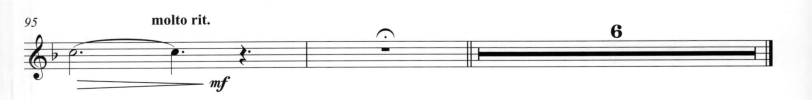

primavera

LUDOVICO **EINAUDI**

una mattina

LUDOVICO **EINAUDI**

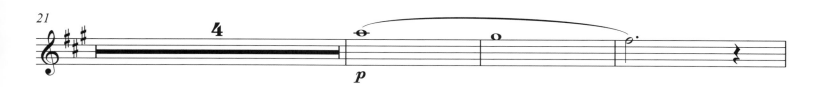

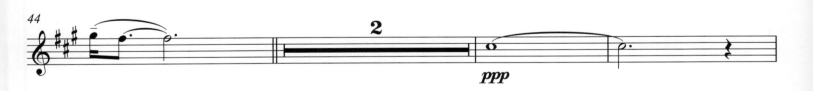

1 2 3 4 5 6 7 8 9

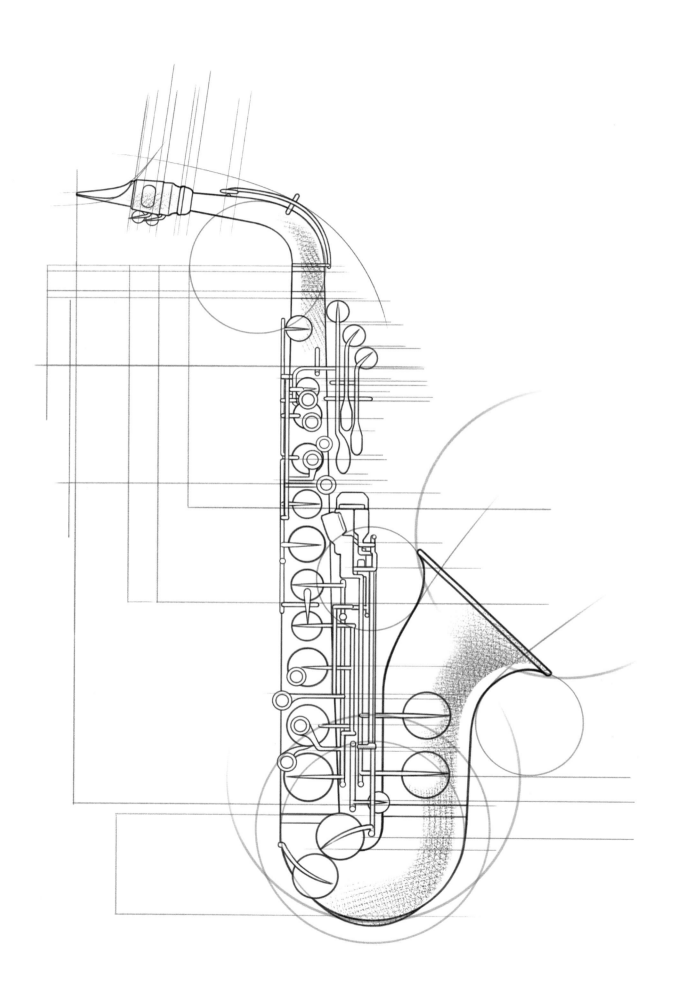

Ludovico EINAUDI

the saxophone collection

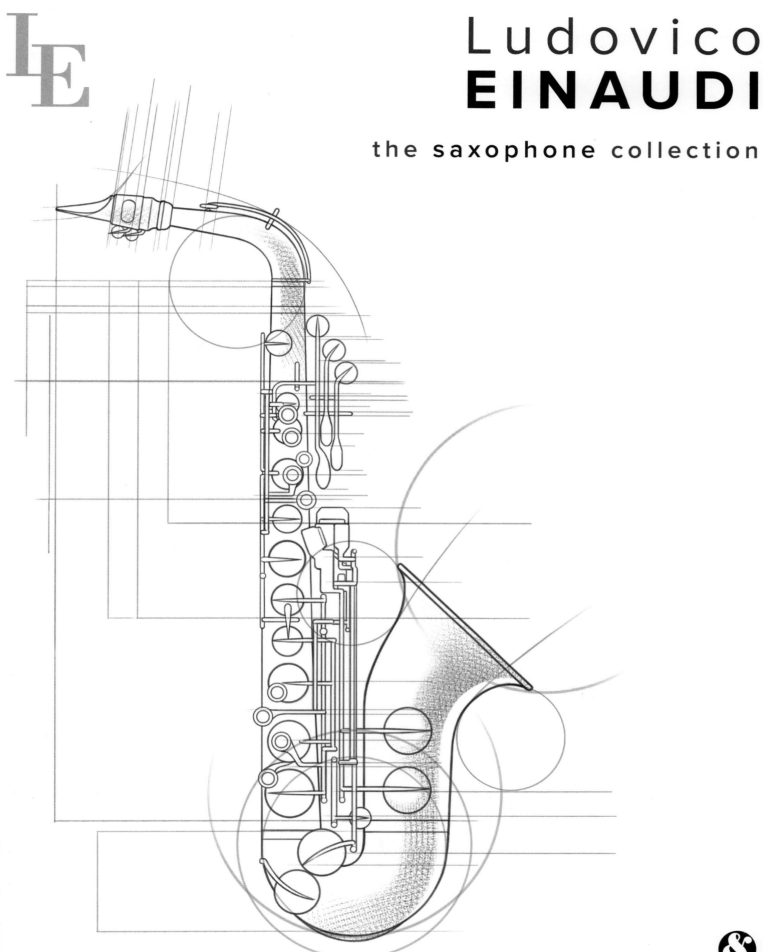

CHESTER MUSIC
part of The Music Sales Group
London/New York/Paris/Sydney/Copenhagen/Berlin/Madrid/Hong Kong/Tokyo

Contents

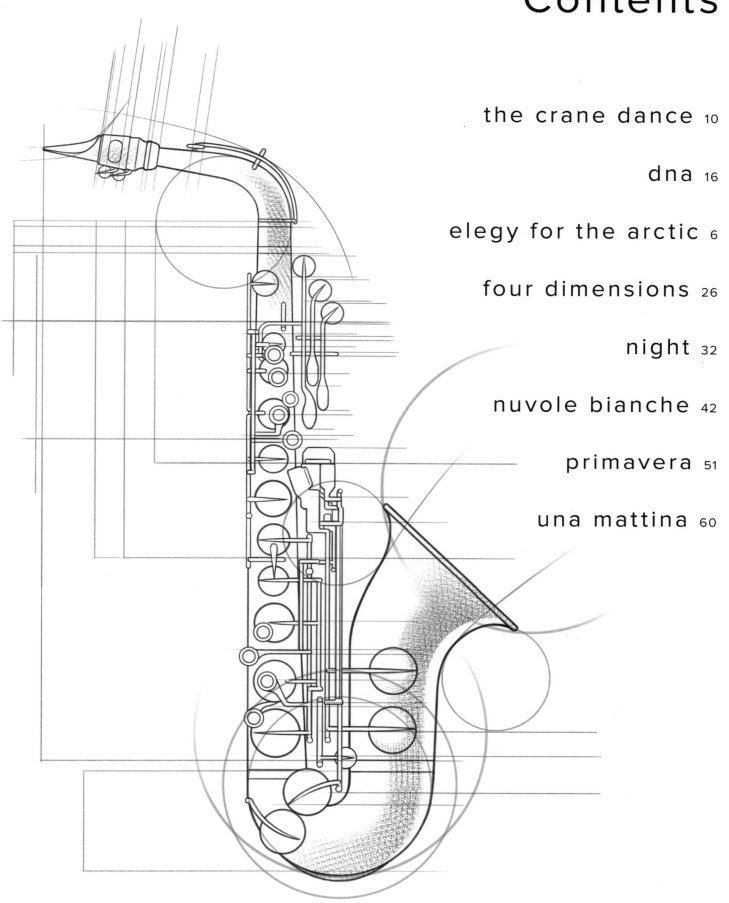

elegy for the arctic

LUDOVICO **EINAUDI**

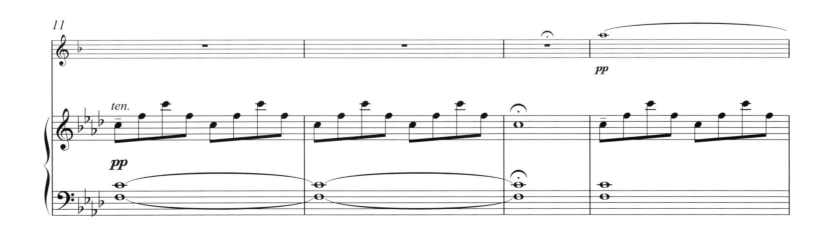

the crane dance

LUDOVICO **EINAUDI**

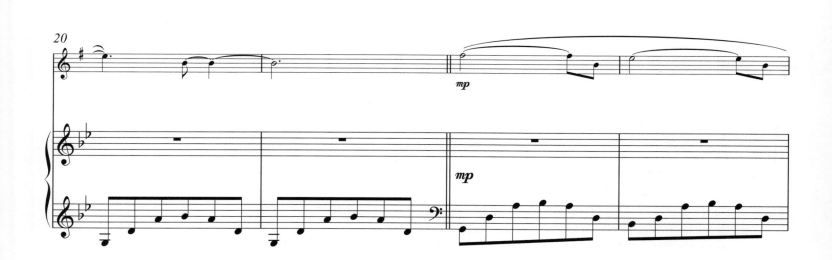

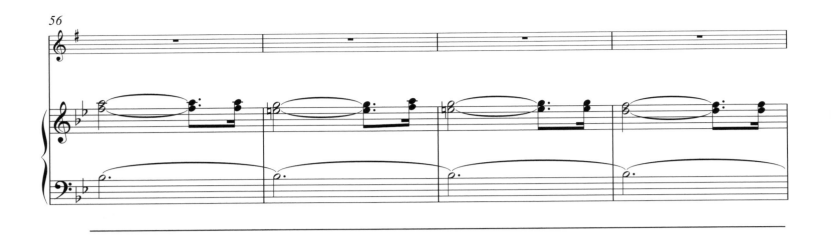

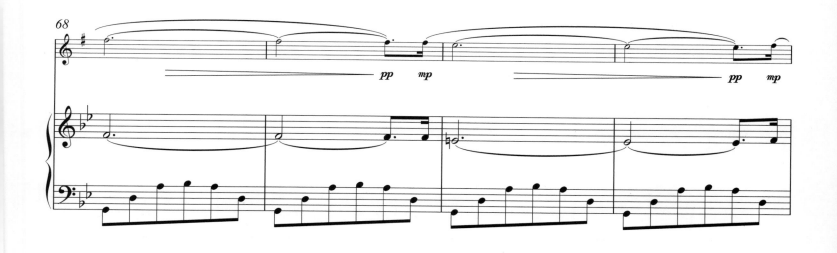

dna

four dimensions

LUDOVICO **EINAUDI**

night

LUDOVICO **EINAUDI**

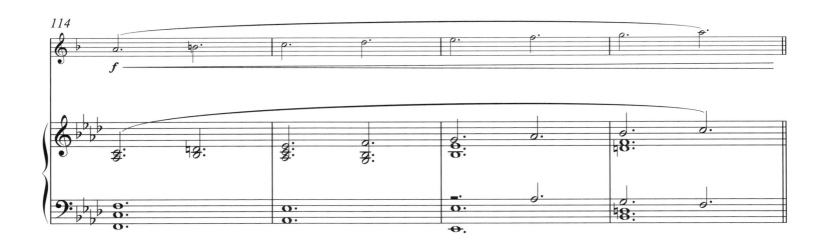

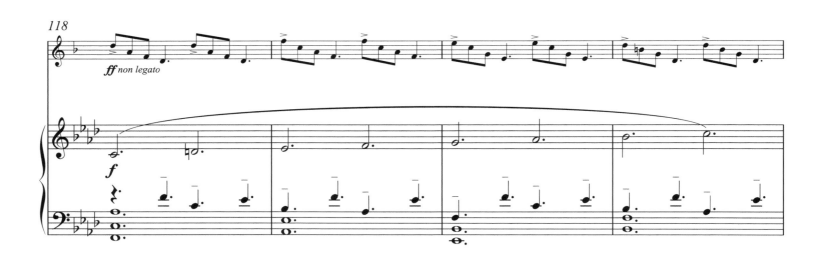

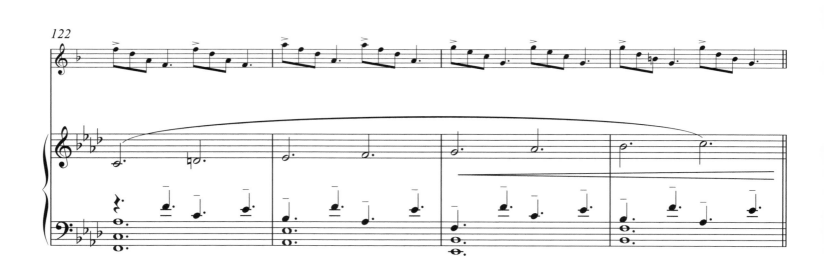

nuvole bianche

LUDOVICO **EINAUDI**

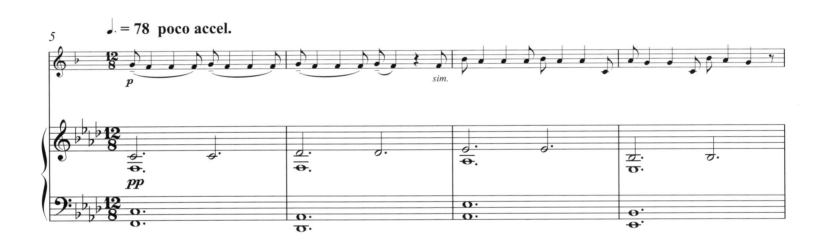

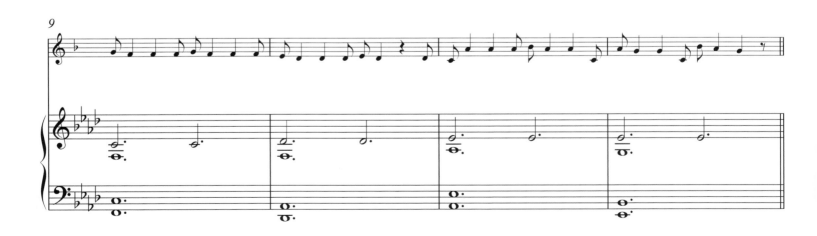

47

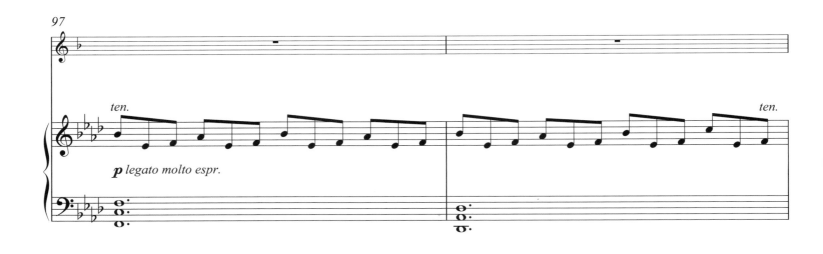

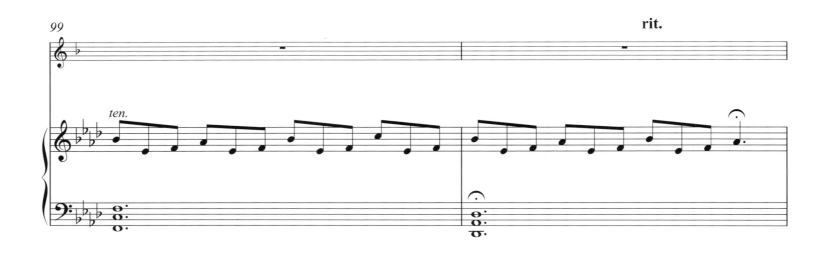

primavera

LUDOVICO **EINAUDI**

55

59

una mattina

LUDOVICO **EINAUDI**